CINDERELLA

Once upon a time, there lived a Baron whose wife died, leaving him to bring up their little girl.

A few years later, when his daughter had grown into a beautiful young lady, the Baron married again. But sadly, soon after, he became ill and died.

His second wife was mean and cruel with a very nasty temper. And to make matters worse, she had two daughters of her own who were even worse than she was. One was very fat, one was very thin and both of them were extremely ugly. In fact, people called them the Ugly Sisters — behind their backs of course!

D0605077

After the Baron's death, his daughter was treated like a servant by the stepmother and her two ugly girls. They forced her to do all the rough work in the house. The poor girl toiled from dawn to dusk, scrubbing floors and washing greasy pots and pans.

The hardest job of all was cleaning out the many fire-grates in the castle. The cinders and soot marked the girl's dress, her hands got grubby and there were black smudges on her nose. That is why the Ugly Sisters unkindly nicknamed her Cinderella.

At night, when all her work was done, Cinderella would sit by the kitchen fire warming her toes near the cinders before she went upstairs to her cold attic room.

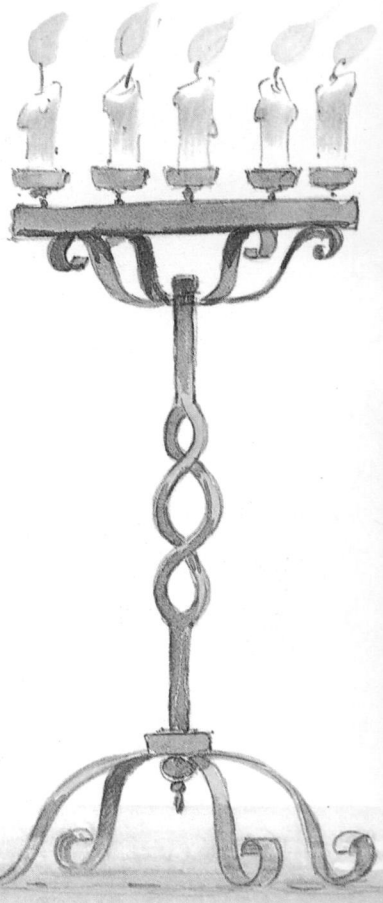

One day at the Royal Palace the King's son announced that he was to give a splendid Ball. To their great joy Cinderella's two step-sisters received an invitation. "You must make us both new ball gowns at once!" one sister yelled at Cinderella. "And do our hair to make us look more beautiful," screeched the other.

This meant that Cinderella had even more work to do. All day long she stitched and sewed. Every pleat, every frill and every bit of lace had to be just right. Not to mention the extra washing, starching and ironing of all their frilly petticoats.

In spite of all the lovely clothes Cinderella had made them, the two sisters still looked dreadfully ugly.

At last the coach arrived to take the Ugly Sisters to the ball. Not one word of thanks did Cinderella get! The nasty pair pushed and shoved their way into their seats, and drove off with their noses in the air.

Sadly, Cinderella went back into the kitchen to sit by the fire. All of a sudden, a log on the fire burst into flames filling the kitchen with light. In the brightness Cinderella noticed, for the first time, a little old lady in a cloak and pointed hat — standing right next to her.

"I am your Fairy Godmother," she said kindly, "and you are going to the Ball!"

Cinderella was too surprised to speak. She had no idea she had a Fairy Godmother.

"Now quickly," the fairy said, "go into the garden and fetch me a pumpkin." Next, she told Cinderella to bring her the six mice and three rats that were caught in the trap near the kitchen cupboard. And last of all, she asked for six lizards from behind the garden shed.

With one wave of her wand the pumpkin was transformed into a glittering golden coach. The six mice turned into fine grey horses. The three rats became handsome coachmen, and lo and behold, the six lizards were smart footmen.

"Well, Cinderella, now you are ready to go to the ball," said her Godmother. "Oh dear, I almost forgot your dress!"

Once more she waved her wand and Cinderella's ragged clothes were changed into a magnificent silver dress which sparkled with precious stones, and there on Cinderella's feet were a pair of glistening glass slippers, which fitted perfectly.

As she was about to drive off in her golden coach, her Godmother called after her, "You must leave the ball before the clock strikes midnight — for my magic only lasts until then." And with a last wave of her wand she vanished.

Cinderella's coach was the last to arrive at the Palace. All the guests in the ballroom turned to look at Cinderella as the Prince stepped forward to greet her.

She danced so well and looked so beautiful that the Prince fell in love with her straight away.

Everyone that night was whispering about the lovely stranger who had captured the heart of the Prince. And Cinderella was so happy she lost all count of time.

All of a sudden the Palace clock struck midnight. Cinderella dashed from the ballroom as fast as she could. Halfway down the grand staircase she lost one of her glass slippers.

As she ran through the Palace gardens her wonderful ballgown turned back into rags.

No golden coach was waiting outside to take her home, instead, lying there on the ground was a pumpkin, and running away were all the mice, the rats and the six lizards.

Cinderella ran back home through the night, and hid in the dark corner of the kitchen. But when she felt in her apron pocket — she found one sparkling glass slipper.

Meanwhile, as the Prince rushed through his Palace searching for her, he found the other slipper on the stairs and picked it up. Desperately the Prince asked every guest at the Ball, and all his servants, but no-one knew the name of the lovely girl.

The very next morning the glass slipper was placed on a velvet cushion and taken to the city square. "I shall marry the girl whose foot fits this glass slipper," announced the Prince.

What excitement this caused! Every girl in the kingdom wanted to try on the slipper. Princesses, serving maids, rich girls, poor girls, all tried — but it was far too small for any of them.

When it came to the Ugly Sisters' turns, they fought and squabbled who should try it on first. They tried their hardest to squeeze their great clumsy feet into the dainty slipper — but it was no use.

All this time Cinderella had been sitting very quietly in the corner. Luckily, the Prince's servant noticed her. He placed the glass slipper on the velvet cushion in front of her. Gently she slipped it on her tiny foot — and it fitted perfectly. Then she took the other slipper from her apron pocket and, of course, they matched.

The Prince was overjoyed to find his lost love and begged Cinderella to be his bride.

The wedding was a splendid affair, with the Fairy Godmother as chief guest. The Ugly Sisters promised to mend their ways — and everyone lived happily ever after.

ALI BABA

Long ago in an eastern land, there lived two brothers, Cassim and Ali Baba. The elder brother Cassim married a very rich wife and didn't have to work at all.

Ali Baba, on the other hand, married a girl as poor as himself, and he had to work very hard for a living. Every day he went to the forest to look for firewood. Then he would load up his donkeys and try to sell his wood in the market place.

One morning while Ali Baba was in the forest chopping wood, he heard the sound of many horses approaching. Now Ali Baba knew there were bands of fierce robbers that roamed the forest — so quickly as possible, he climbed up the nearest tree for safety. Instead of thundering by, as Ali Baba expected, all forty robbers came to a sudden halt. Quickly they dismounted and tethered their horses next to the very spot where Ali Baba was hiding.

The leader of the robbers strode up to a nearby rock and said in a loud voice, "Open sesame!" At these words a door in the rock swung open leading to a cave beyond. One by one the forty thieves disappeared inside, carrying with them huge sacks of silver and gold they had unloaded from their horses. The door slammed shut after the last robber had stepped inside. Poor Ali Baba dared not climb down from his hiding place for fear of his life.

After what seemed a very long uncomfortable wait, the forty thieves came out of the cave empty-handed. The robber chief raised his arms and cried, "Close sesame!" and the door in the rock shut tight. The robbers jumped back on their horses and rode away.

Plucking up all his courage, Ali Baba jumped down from the tree and ran over to the rock. "Open sesame!" he cried in a trembling voice. Straight away, the door swung open and Ali Baba found himself in a gigantic cave.

What wonders met his eyes! Sacks full of silver and gold, priceless carpets, ornaments of ivory and jade and endless chests of precious jewels. Hurriedly, Ali Baba grabbed a couple of the bags of gold, ran out of the cave, and loaded up his donkeys.

When Ali Baba's wife saw all that gold, she was overjoyed. "It is far too much to count," she whispered quite breathless. "We must measure it into small sacks and hide it, for if we spend it a little at a time, no-one will suspect we have the robbers' gold."

So off she ran to the elder brother, Cassim's house to borrow a measure. This made Cassim's wife very suspicious. "Ali Baba's wife is far too poor to need a measure," she thought to herself. So secretly she stuck a small piece of wax to the bottom — so that whatever was put in the measure would stick.

Sure enough when the measure was returned next day, one shiny gold coin was stuck to the wax. It really puzzled Cassim and his wife.

The following morning, Ali Baba set out as usual for the forest. But this time his brother Cassim was following him secretly. As soon as Ali Baba reached the rock, he uttered the magic words, "Open sesame!" the door opened and he stepped inside. Very soon he reappeared loaded down with gold and jewels.

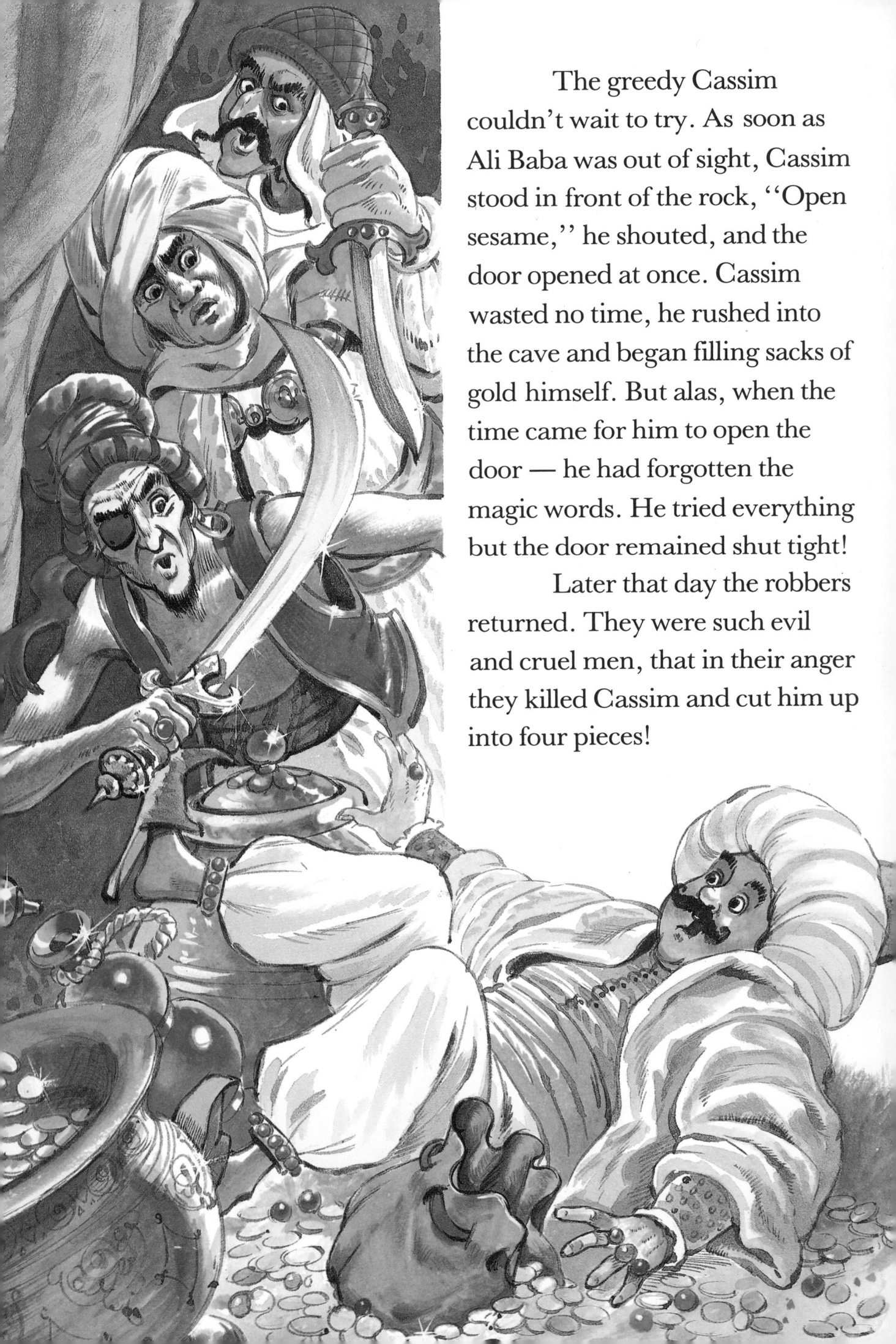

The greedy Cassim couldn't wait to try. As soon as Ali Baba was out of sight, Cassim stood in front of the rock, "Open sesame," he shouted, and the door opened at once. Cassim wasted no time, he rushed into the cave and began filling sacks of gold himself. But alas, when the time came for him to open the door — he had forgotten the magic words. He tried everything but the door remained shut tight!

Later that day the robbers returned. They were such evil and cruel men, that in their anger they killed Cassim and cut him up into four pieces!

Late that night when Cassim didn't return, his wife told Ali Baba how Cassim had followed him into the forest to spy on him. Ali Baba guessed what had happened. In the middle of the night he returned to the robbers' cave and found his poor dead brother just inside the entrance.

He loaded the four pieces of the body onto his donkey and returned home to break the terrible news to Cassim's wife. After much weeping, the family decided that Cassim's body must be sewn together before he could be buried (that way no-one would know he had been cut into pieces by the thieves).

A faithful family slave called Morgiana knew of an old blind cobbler who could do the task. In the dead of night she led the old man to Cassim's house. Skilfully he stitched the four pieces together, so no-one would know that Cassim had not died in his sleep. As soon as he had finished, Morgiana led him back home through the dark city streets.

Meanwhile, the forty thieves returned to their cave. When they found that Cassim's body had vanished they realised someone else knew of their hiding place. They rode into the city and began to question everyone. It wasn't long before the blind cobbler told them of his unusual task the night before.

Although he was blind, he could easily remember the path that led to Cassim's house. The leader of the thieves marked the door with a large cross — so his men could return later and kill everyone inside. But clever Morgiana came along and marked every door in the street with a cross to confuse the thieves — and their evil plan was foiled.

All too soon, the robber chief heard about Ali Baba, who had once been a poor woodcutter, and was now the richest man in the city. It didn't take him long to guess it was Ali Baba who knew the secret of their cave.

So, the leader of the robbers disguised himself as a merchant selling oil. He called at Ali Baba's house asking for a night's lodging. With him he had a team of donkeys, each one loaded with a great jar. In every jar was hiding one of his evil band. Only one of the jars contained oil. That night when the household was fast asleep, the thieves planned to jump out and kill everyone.

Quite by chance, Morgiana ran out of oil for cooking. "I will borrow a little from the Merchant's jar," she thought to herself.

It was then she discovered the thieves' trick. The cunning girl filled a huge pan full of oil from the jar and heated it up on the stove. When it was boiling hot she tipped some into every jar — and the forty thieves were scalded to death.